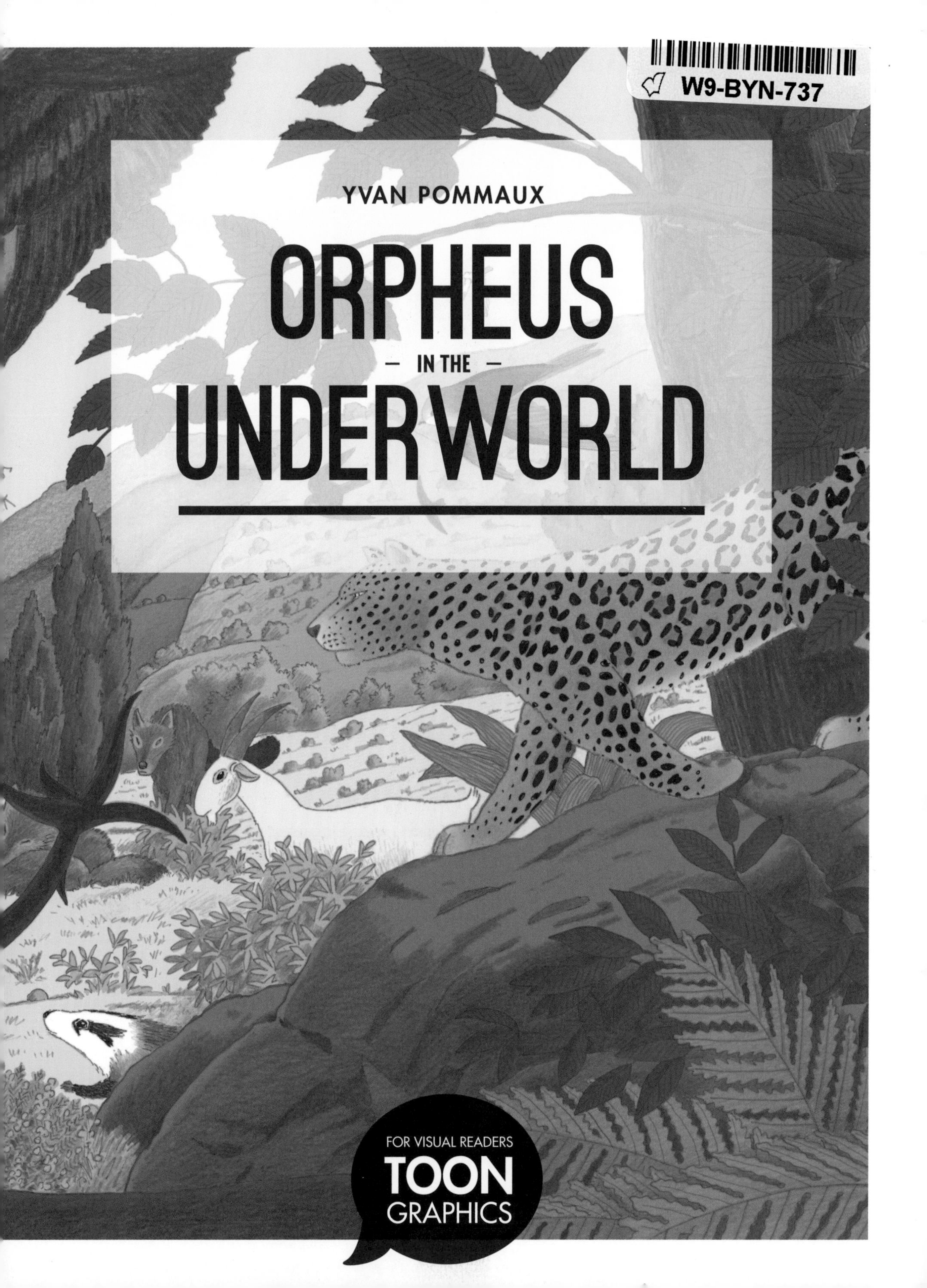

YVAN POMMAUX

ORPHEUS IN THE UNDERWORLD

FOR VISUAL READERS
TOON GRAPHICS

Editorial Direction & Book Design: FRANÇOISE MOULY

Deputy Editor & Production: SASHA STEINBERG

Editorial Consultant: DASH

Coloring: NICOLE POMMAUX

YVAN POMMAUX'S artwork was drawn in pencil and india ink and colored digitally.

A JUNIOR LIBRARY GUILD SELECTION

 All our books are Smyth Sewn (the highest library-quality binding available) and printed with soy-based inks on acid-free, woodfree paper harvested from responsible sources. Printed in Shenzhen, China by Imago. Distributed to the trade by Consortium Book Sales and Distribution, Inc.; orders (800) 283-3572 34; orderentry@perseusbooks.com; www.cbsd.com.
Library of Congress Cataloging-in-Publication Data:
Pommaux, Yvan, author, illustrator. [Orphée et la morsure du serpent. English] Orpheus in the underworld / Yvan Pommaux; translated by Richard Kutner. pages cm. -- (TOON Graphic Mythology)
ISBN 978-1-935179-84-9 1. Orpheus (Greek mythological character)--Comic books, strips, etc. 2. Orpheus (Greek mythological character)--Juvenile literature. 3. Eurydice (Greek mythological character)--Comic books, strips, etc. 4. Eurydice (Greek mythological character)--Juvenile literature. 5. Graphic novels. I. Kutner, Richard, translator. II. Title. BL820.O7P6613 2015 741.5'944--dc23 2014028862

ISBN 978-1-935179-84-9 (hardcover)

15 16 17 18 19 20 IMG 10 9 8 7 6 5 4 3 2 1

WWW.TOON-BOOKS.COM

YVAN POMMAUX

ORPHEUS
— IN THE —
UNDERWORLD

A TOON GRAPHIC

Translated by RICHARD KUTNER

GATHER AROUND AND HEAR THE TALE OF ORPHEUS AND EURYDICE, TWO STAR-CROSSED LOVERS WHO EXPERIENCED THE GREATEST LOVE AND THE DEEPEST SORROW.

THIS IS AN ANCIENT STORY, KEPT ALIVE BY THE BARDS WHO SANG OF IT AGAIN AND AGAIN. THIS HEROIC TALE CHANGES WITH EACH RETELLING- BUT THAT IS HOW MYTHS ARE BORN.

The great gods and goddesses of Ancient Greece lived on Mount Olympus*, a realm above the clouds where they could look down upon mortals going about their daily lives.

* O·LYM·PUS [o-***lim***-puss]

Zeus* and Hera,* mightiest of all the gods, spent their days being entertained by the Muses,* nine beautiful sisters who inspired song, poetry, and the other arts. Apollo,* god of light and music, accompanied them on his magnificent turtle-shell lyre.*

One day, Calliope,* Muse of epic poetry, fell in love with a mortal, the king of Thrace,* and decided she must have him for her own. She came down to earth, and soon Orpheus* was born.

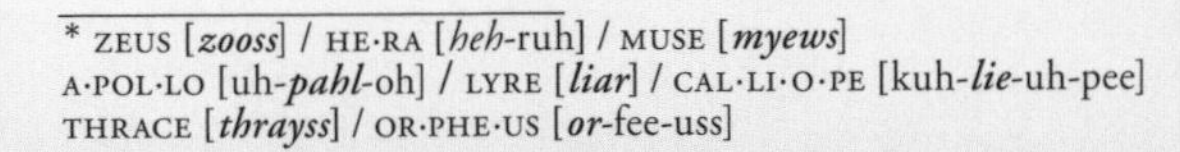
* ZEUS [*zooss*] / HE·RA [*heh*-ruh] / MUSE [*myews*]
A·POL·LO [uh-*pahl*-oh] / LYRE [*liar*] / CAL·LI·O·PE [kuh-*lie*-uh-pee]
THRACE [*thrayss*] / OR·PHE·US [*or*-fee-uss]

As one of the nine muses, Calliope soon had to return to Olympus to entertain the other gods. But before she left, she asked Apollo to give his turtle-shell lyre to her son Orpheus.

Longing for his mother, the lonely boy practiced day and night. Calliope's divine gift granted him many powerful abilities.

The wind would follow him, whistling in harmony with his music.

His song was so beautiful that the most ferocious beasts would lie calmly at his feet to listen.

Rocks and boulders rolled down hills to be closer to him and...

...stiff trees bent to brush against him.

Even raging rivers stilled themselves
to catch his reflection.

SPLISH!

SPLASH!

It should be no surprise that all the women of Thrace were head over heels in love with this handsome young poet. Unfortunately for them, their expressions of ardor fell on deaf ears.

One evening, Orpheus was performing for an audience that had traveled far to hear him sing, when suddenly he was struck by the most beautiful pair of eyes he had ever seen, shining up at him.

He knew then that he must have this woman for his own, and he begged her to come with him.

EURYDICE?* WHAT A **BEAUTIFUL** NAME.

IT SOUNDS EVEN BETTER WHEN ***YOU*** SAY IT.

* EU·RYD·I·CE [you-*rid*-i-see]

Quickly, the two of them fell in love.

Son of a muse, he regaled her with the stories of the gods.

* PER·SEPH·O·NE [per-*seff*-oh-nee]

Their love grew and grew...

...and it wasn't long before they were wed.

Their happiness was to be short-lived, however, as the Three Fates had other plans for the two lovers.

The first Fate spun life into long threads, the second measured out how long the thread of each life should be, and the third made the cut that signified death.

Meanwhile, back at the wedding, the beautiful bride had attracted eyes other than Orpheus's; Aristaeus, son of Apollo* and the huntress Cyrene,* had intruded on the festivities and began pursuing Eurydice.

* A·RIS·TAE·ES [a-ris-*tee*-iss] / CY·RE·NE [sigh-*ree*-nee]

Eurydice hurried away from the unwanted pursuer…
…and towards her fate.

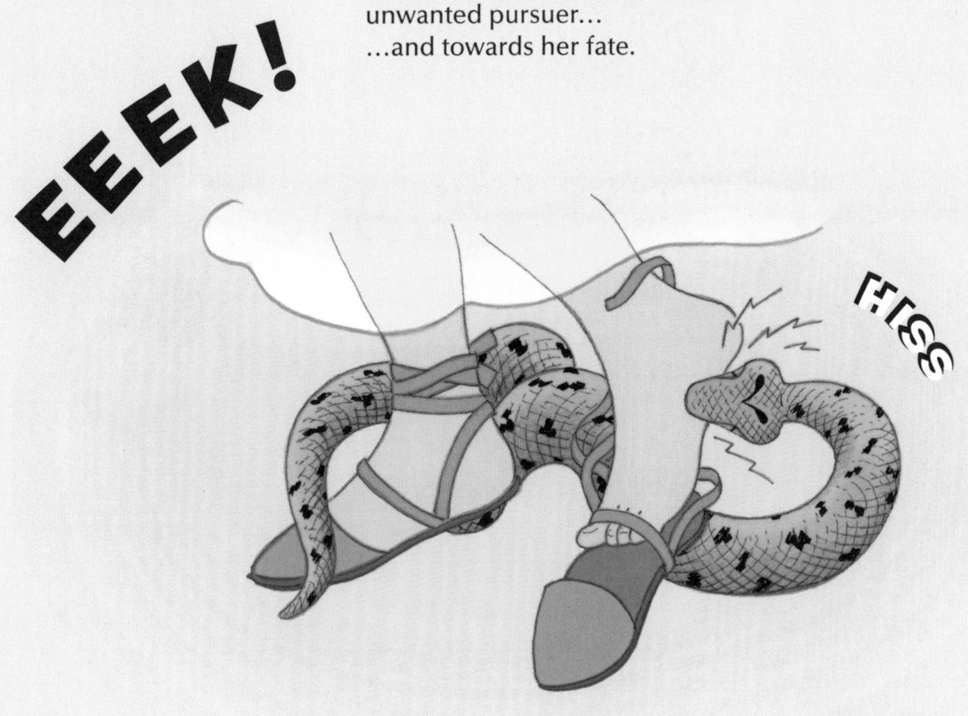

She stepped on a snake that sank its fang into her foot.

The snake's bite was fatal. Orpheus held his beloved as she died in his arms.

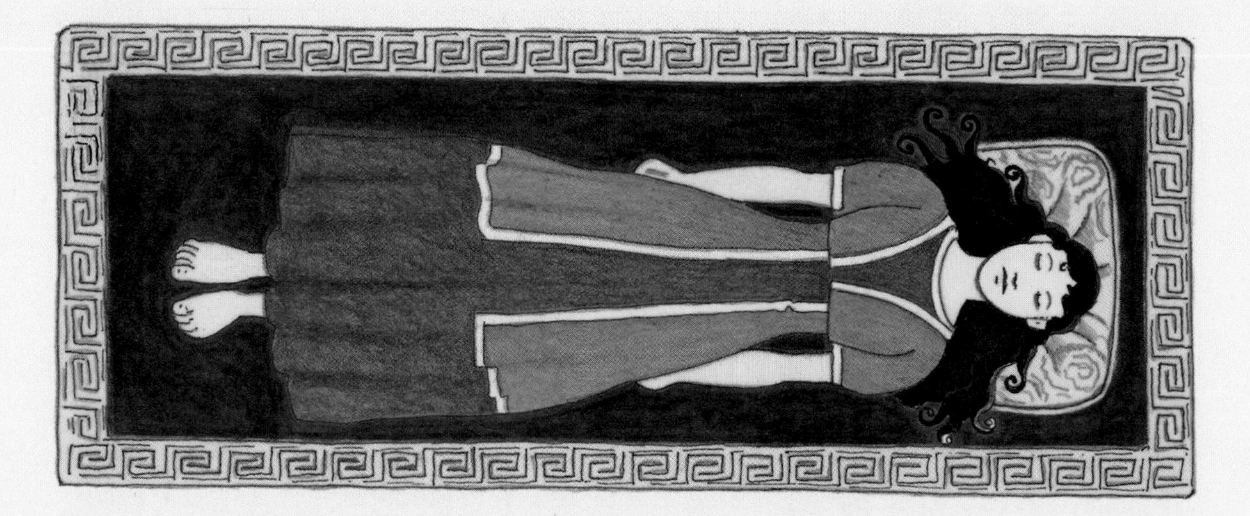

He made sure no expense was spared on Eurydice's funeral. She was laid on the finest silks, and a gold coin was placed beneath her tongue.

After the lavish burial, Orpheus left his father's kingdom to mourn his loss out in the wilds. The world had never seen such sorrow.

I'LL FOLLOW
THE BIRDS...
...SEARCHING
FOR MY
EURYDICE...

Orpheus set foot in the Underworld, the realm of Hades, where no mortal had ventured before.

* HA·DES [*hay*-deez]

Arriving at the end of a long, narrow passageway, Orpheus discovered a gloomy landscape. He walked along a marsh that flowed into a dark lake. Nothing was stirring.

EVERYTHING'S SO STILL. AND WHAT AN UNCANNY SILENCE!

* STYX [*sticks*] / CHAR·ON [*kar*-un]

In front of Orpheus were the lost souls – those whose families had forgotten to put a gold coin beneath their tongue during their burial. They would have to wait one hundred years for the greedy ferryman, Charon,* to take them to their final resting place.

Once they managed the crossing, the good souls departed for the lush Elysian Fields,* where they remained happy for eternity, and the bad ones were shut away in the terrible abyss of Tartarus,* where they suffered torments forever.

Charon was known for being irascible and short-tempered, and he ferried only the dead. When he started to object, however, Orpheus started to play.

Charon did not even ask for gold. Orpheus's soulful songs were payment enough for him.

* E·LY·SIAN FIELDS [uh-*lee*-zhun feelds] / TAR·TA·RUS [*tar*-tuh-russ]

THANK YOU, MY FRIEND.

NO, THANK ***YOU***! THESE OLD EARS HAD ***ALMOST*** FORGOTTEN THE SOUND OF MUSIC.

Orpheus came upon the fierce three-headed dog Cerberus,* who stood watch over everyone who entered the underworld.

* CER·BER·US [*sur*-bur-us]

But it turned out that even monsters were not immune
to Orpheus's enchanting music.

SLEEP WELL,
GENTLE PUP.

The land of the dead was littered with the tortured souls of those who had committed crimes against the gods:

Sisyphus* labored to push a giant boulder up a mountain, only to have it roll back down just before he reached the top.

Tantalus* starved, with succulent fruits dangling just out of his reach.

Tityos* tried to fend off the vicious vultures that daily devoured his entrails, which grew back every night.

The Danaides* went over and over again to the river, filling barrels pierced with holes.

* SIS·Y·PHUS [*siss*-uh-fiss]
TAN·TA·LUS [*tan*-tuh-luss]
TIT·YOS [*tit*-yohss]
DA·NA·I·DES [da-*nay*-ih-deez]

At last, Orpheus came to the palace of Hades, god of the Underworld.

Orpheus came upon the cold-hearted Hades and his queen, Persephone, seated on a throne with treelike branches sculpted in the rock. They remained silent as they stared icily at the intruder.

Orpheus began to sing. He sang of his undying love for his dear Eurydice and of the pain it caused him to be apart from her. He sang of his love, and it was as if no one had ever loved before him.

The melody that begged for Eurydice swelled, filled the palace, made the stone vibrate, and pierced the hearts of those who heard it. Then he gradually grew silent.

The tender-hearted Persephone, who was forced by Hades to spend each winter with him, away from all the things she loved most, was greatly moved by Orpheus's song.

The king gestured to Thanatos* and Hypnos,* the spirits of Death and Sleep, who went to get Eurydice and led her to the throne. But it wasn't really Eurydice. It was her ghost, and Orpheus felt his heart sink. Eurydice's eyes were empty, like those of the beings who wandered along the banks of the River Styx.

* THA·NA·TOS [*than*-uh-tohss] / HYP·NOS [*hip*-nohss]

Hades agreed to let Eurydice return to earth with Orpheus on one condition.

The way back was longer and more treacherous than the way down, and little seeds of doubt were growing in Orpheus's mind...

Would she still love him as he loved her? Had death and her time in the Underworld changed her forever?

Were those her footsteps he heard faintly behind him? Was that her breath he could feel ever so lightly on his neck?

Had Hades tricked him? Was it all a ploy to get him to leave?

He could just begin to see the warm light of the world above shining down into the tunnel. He couldn't stand his doubts anymore – he just ***had*** to check. He turned around...

He had one final glimpse
of his beloved as her
ghostly form descended
back into the Underworld.

He tried in vain to follow her, to catch her agai

and get a second chance, but Charon turned him away.

Hades' word was final; Eurydice would never leave the Underworld again.

There was no hope or joy left for Orpheus.

Filled with guilt and shame at what he had done, he wandered the earth, pining for his lost Eurydice.

The other women of Thrace grew bitter, since Orpheus sang only of Eurydice and paid no attention to them. One day, in a jealous rage, they threw themselves upon him and tore him apart. In their clamor, they were unable to hear his voice.

They threw Orpheus's lyre and the pieces of his body in the river, which carried them to the sea. The currents carried them to the isle of Lesbos.* There, on the sand, Orpheus's head was still singing.

* LES·BOS [*lez*-bohss]

Seeing Orpheus's sad end, the Muses came down and reclaimed his body. They buried him at the foot of Mount Olympus, where the song of the nightingale was more beautiful than anywhere else. They gave him a proper burial so that his soul could return to the Underworld.

And, at long last, Orpheus was reunited with his beloved Eurydice.

SINGING HERO

Orpheus (Ὀρφεύς)

Meaning of the name:

The darkness of the night

Place of birth: Pimpleia, near Mount Olympus

Father: King Oeagrus of Thrace

Mother: Calliope, Muse of Epic Poetry

Siblings: Linus

Wife: Eurydice

LOVING SPIRIT

Eurydice (Εὐρυδίκη)

Meaning of the name:

Far-reaching justice

Place of birth: The forest

Mother: Oak tree (Eurydice is a dryad, a female tree spirit that is born from an oak tree and is often known for being shy.)

Husband: Orpheus

RULER OF THE UNDERWORLD

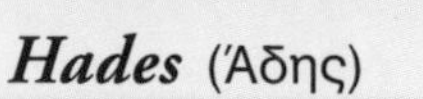

Hades (Ἅδης)

Meaning of the name:

Unseen

Place of birth: Mount Olympus

Father: Cronos

Mother: Rhea

Siblings: Poseidon, Demeter, Hestia, Hera, Zeus

Children: Macaria, Melinoe, and Zagreus

PLANT GODDESS

Persephone (Περσεφόνη)

Also called:

Kore, "The maiden"

Persephone is both the goddess of Spring and queen of the Underworld.

Place of birth: Mount Olympus

Father: Zeus, king of the gods

Mother: Demeter, goddess of the Harvest

Husband: Hades

FERRYMAN OF DEATH

Charon (Χάρων)

Meaning of the name:
Of keen gaze

Father: Erebus, the personification of darkness

Mother: Nyx, goddess of the Night

Siblings: Aether, Moros, Hypnos, Keres, Thanatos, Momus, Hemera, Nemesis, Ponos, Limos, Usmine, Mache, Phonos, Pseudea

DEMON OF DEATH

Cerberus (Κέρβερος)

Meaning of the name:
Spotted

Father: Typhon, a fire-breathing giant covered with dragons and serpents.

Mother: Echidna, a creature who was half-woman, half-serpent

MUSE OF EPIC POETRY

Calliope (Καλλιόπη)

Meaning of the name:
Beautiful voice

Place of birth: Mount Olympus

Father: Zeus

Mother: Mnemosyne

Siblings: The Muses: Clio, Erato, Euterpe, Melpomene, Polyhymnia, Terpischore, Thalia, Urania

Children: Orpheus and Linus

DECIDERS OF DESTINY

The Fates (Μοίραι)

Meaning of the name:
Apportioners

Names: Clotho (spinner), Lachesis (measurer), Atropos (cutter)

Father: Zeus

Mother: Themis

INDEX

ARISTAEUS—Son of Apollo *(see below)*, he was a demi-god, protector of cattle and fruit trees. He invented olive oil and hydromel (a drink made with water and honey). Most of all, he loved to keep bees. Aristaeus was involuntarily responsible for the death of Eurydice, and his punishment was the destruction of all his bees. He had to sacrifice four bulls and four cows to be able to repopulate his beehives *(p. 24-25)*.

APOLLO—Son of Zeus *(see right)* and Leto. His twin sister was Artemis. He was the god of the arts, music, healing, prophecy, intelligence, and archery. He also showed men the art of medicine. Both Apollo and Artemis had power over the plague. He was famous for his oracle at Delphi, to which people traveled from all over the Greek world to learn their future *(p. 11-12, 24)*.

THE BARDS—Bards were Ancient Greek poet-singer-musicians. Orpheus, a legendary figure with the irresistible power to captivate whoever heard him, was the most famous of the bards *(p. 8)*.

CALLIOPE—Orpheus's mother and one of the nine beautiful daughters of Zeus called the Muses *(see right)*. Together they created entertainment for the sometimes boring leisure time of the gods and goddesses of Olympus. Each Muse had her own specialty. Calliope's were poetry and eloquence, which she transmitted to her son, Orpheus (*p. 11-13)*.

CERBERUS—Beware of the dog! Cerberus had three heads bristling with snakes with venomous fangs. Guardian of the Underworld, he prevented the condemned from escaping and decided who could enter *(p. 36-37, 45)*.

CHARON—A disagreeable, rude, greedy old man who ferried the dead across the River Styx. Beyond this river lay the Underworld. To pay for the dead person's passage, loved ones had to place gold coins called oboles under the tongue. If they forgot, Charon made the dead one wait one hundred years. Of course, he refused to ferry curious living people *(p. 33-36, 45-47)*.

THE DANAIDES—Enclosed in bronze walls, Tartarus *(see right)* was the part of the Underworld where wicked people had to suffer eternal torment for their misdeeds. Here labored the Danaides, the fifty daughters of the mythical Egyptian king Danaus. Because of family conflicts, they had killed their fifty husbands on their wedding night. Zeus condemned the Danaides to spend the rest of time filling barrels with water, which immediately spilled out of holes bored in them *(p. 39)*.

THE ELYSIAN FIELDS—The part of the Underworld where the virtuous enjoyed eternity among lush greenery. It is the equivalent of the Christian idea of Heaven. People could go there only if they deserved to, with access controlled by Cerberus *(p. 34)*.

EURYDICE—A beautiful nymph (a sort of second-class divinity, but a divinity just the same). Orpheus *(see right)* fell head over heels in love with her, which was why he was so distraught when he lost her. He didn't hesitate to descend to the Underworld to retrieve her. Alas, his impatience caused his quest to end in failure *(p. 19-28, 41-47)*.

THE FATES— Three sisters who spun, tangled, and cut the threads of human destinies. Some people say they lived in a palace on Mount Olympus, while others say they dwelled in a cave in the Underworld. (Everyone agrees, though, that they controlled people's fate) *(p. 22-23)*.

HADES—The brother of Zeus *(see right)* and god of the Underworld. His palace was in the center of Tartarus *(see right)*, where he reigned surrounded by ghosts *(p. 29, 40-48)*.

HERA— Hera is Zeus's wife *(see right)*. She was raised by the Titans Ocean and Tethys. The supreme goddess, she protected marriage and childbirth and took special care of married women *(p. 11)*.

HYPNOS—Son of the Night and spirit of sleep, Hypnos was the twin brother of Thanatos *(see right)*, spirit of death. He lived in a dark place planted with poppies (think of the effect of the poppy field in the Wizard of Oz), although no one knows exactly where. He spent his time relaxing on his ebony bed, dispensing life-giving sleep to mortals *(p. 42)*.

LESBOS—An island in the Aegean Sea. Known for the free and open attitudes of its inhabitants, the Isle of Lesbos was home to the famous female Greek poet, Sappho *(p. 48)*.

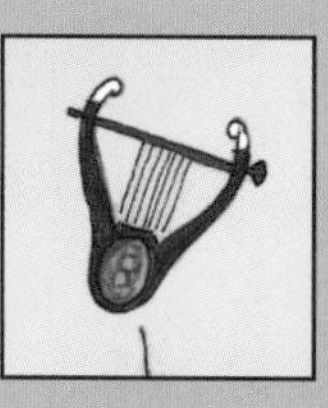

LYRE— A stringed instrument consisting of a soundbox (a vibrating membrane often made from the skin of an ox or kid stretched over the open side of a turtle shell), two arms (made of goat horns or two similar curved wooden rods) and a crossbar *(p. 8, 11-20, 27-49)*.

MOUNT OLYMPUS—The enchanted world above the clouds where the Greek gods and goddesses dwelled, enclosed in a citadel with phantom portals. The gods and goddesses were ruled by Zeus *(see right) (p. 10-11, 49)*.

THE MUSES—Daughters of Zeus, these nine young and beautiful sisters amused and stimulated the gods, who were at leisure for eternity. Each had her own specialty: singing, dance, drama, poetry, etc. They always kept the gods amused with high-quality entertainment *(p. 11, 49).*

ORPHEUS—Hero of this book. Orpheus was the model of the passionate, faithful lover. Because he could not save his beautiful wife, Eurydice *(see left)*, from the Underworld, he was an inconsolable widower, who showed no interest in any of the other women of Thrace. A victim of his own loyalty to Eurydice, he was torn to pieces by a group of jealous women *(p. 8, 11-49).*

PERSEPHONE—The goddess of Spring. She was kidnapped by Hades *(see left)* to the dismay of her mother, Demeter, goddess of the harvest. Demeter's anger was so fierce that she froze every plant on earth. Zeus made a compromise with his brother, Hades. Hades would let Persephone return to earth, but since she had eaten pomegranate seeds in the Underworld, she would have to return one month for every seed she ate. *(p. 20, 41-43).*

THE RIVER STYX—The best known of the rivers of the Underworld. The Styx was muddy and made many meanders around the domain of the dead. Its waters made anyone who entered them invulnerable *(p. 32-35, 43-45).*

SISYPHUS—A prince who betrayed Zeus. His punishment was to roll a huge rock up to the top of a mountain forever. He always lost his grip, and the rock rolled back down the slope *(p. 39).*

TANTALUS—His crime was stealing ambrosia and nectar, food and drink reserved for the gods. As his punishment, he was forced to spend all eternity suffering from hunger and thirst, next to fruits and drinks just out of his reach *(p. 39).*

TARTARUS—The part of the Underworld where people were punished for their crimes, especially the bold ones who offended Zeus *(p. 44-47).*

THANATOS—Spirit of death, Thanatos was the twin brother of Hypnos (*see left,* spirit of sleep) and son of the Night. Thanatos was violent and inflexible and was detested by everyone. He lived in Tartarus and wouldn't go out unless he was wearing a black veil. He carried a scythe in his hand *(p. 42).*

THRACE—A region in the north of Ancient Greece and the home of Orpheus *(p. 11, 18, 48).*

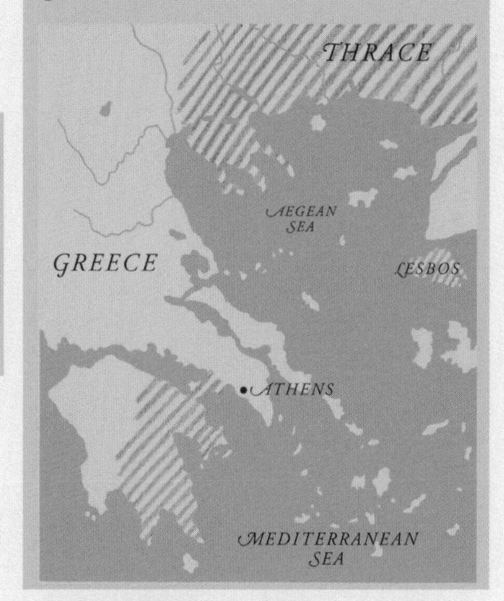

TITYOS— A brutal giant whom Apollo killed to prevent him from causing any more harm. His eternal punishment was to suffer attacks by two vultures determined to devour his liver *(p. 39).*

ZEUS—Having already defeated the Titans and removed his father, Saturn, from his throne, Zeus became the king of the gods, governing the sky and the earth. He gave his power over the sea to Poseidon and entrusted the Underworld to Hades *(see left) (p. 11).*

FURTHER READING & RESOURCES.

Ancient Greek myths come to us from an oral tradition, told by people for centuries before they were written down. Storytellers over the ages varied details. This book is one version of the myth of Orpheus in the Underworld–you may see it told differently elsewhere. Here is a list of other books you might enjoy:

D'AULAIRES' BOOK OF GREEK MYTHS; Ingri and Edgar Parin D'Aulaire. Doubleday, 1962. *Still the best introductory book to Greek mythology. Ages 8+*

MYTHOLOGY: TIMELESS TALES OF GODS AND HEROES; Edith Hamilton. Back Bay Books, 2013. *A reissue of Hamilton's original 1942 book–the number one mythology book for older readers. Ages 14+*

HEROES, GODS, AND MONSTERS OF THE GREEK MYTHS; Bernard Evslin. Laurel Leaf, 1984. *Middle school level. Ages 12+*

GREEK GODS AND HEROES; Robert Graves. Laurel Leaf, 1965. *Retellings of the Greek myths that entertain and convey information. Ages 12+*

MYTHOLOGY: THE GODS, HEROES, AND MONSTERS OF ANCIENT GREECE (OLOGIES); Lady Hestia Evans, Dugald A. Steer, and various. Candlewick, 2007. *An interactive book about the Greek myths. Ages 8+*

GREEK MYTHS; Olivia E. Coolidge. Houghton Mifflin Harcourt, 2001. *A text that categorizes stories by theme, such as Loves of the Gods, Men's Rivalry with Gods, and Adventure Stories. Ages 12+*

GREEK MYTHS; Ann Turnbull. Candlewick, 2010. *A lively retelling of the Greek myths by a modern author. Ages 10+*

Online Resources:

WWW.THEOI.COM *A very well-researched encyclopedia of gods and goddesses from Greek mythology.*

WWW.SACRED-TEXTS.COM/CLA/BULF *Bulfinch's Greek and Roman Mythology. Thomas Bulfinch was an American scholar who compiled tales of mythology from both Ovid and Virgil. His work is now in the public domain and is available online at this URL.*

WWW.PANTHEON.ORG *This encyclopedia of mythology provides a reference guide to not only Greek mythology, but to mythology and folklore from Africa, the Americas, Asia, Europe, the Middle East, and Oceania.*

WWW.HISTORY.COM/TOPICS/GREEK-MYTHOLOGY *The History Channel has great video guides to the heroes and gods.*

THE
RIVER STYX
CHARON'S
FERRY
LAND OF
LOST SOULS
CERBERUS
A MAP
OF THE
UNDER-
WORLD
Map by SASHA STEINBERG

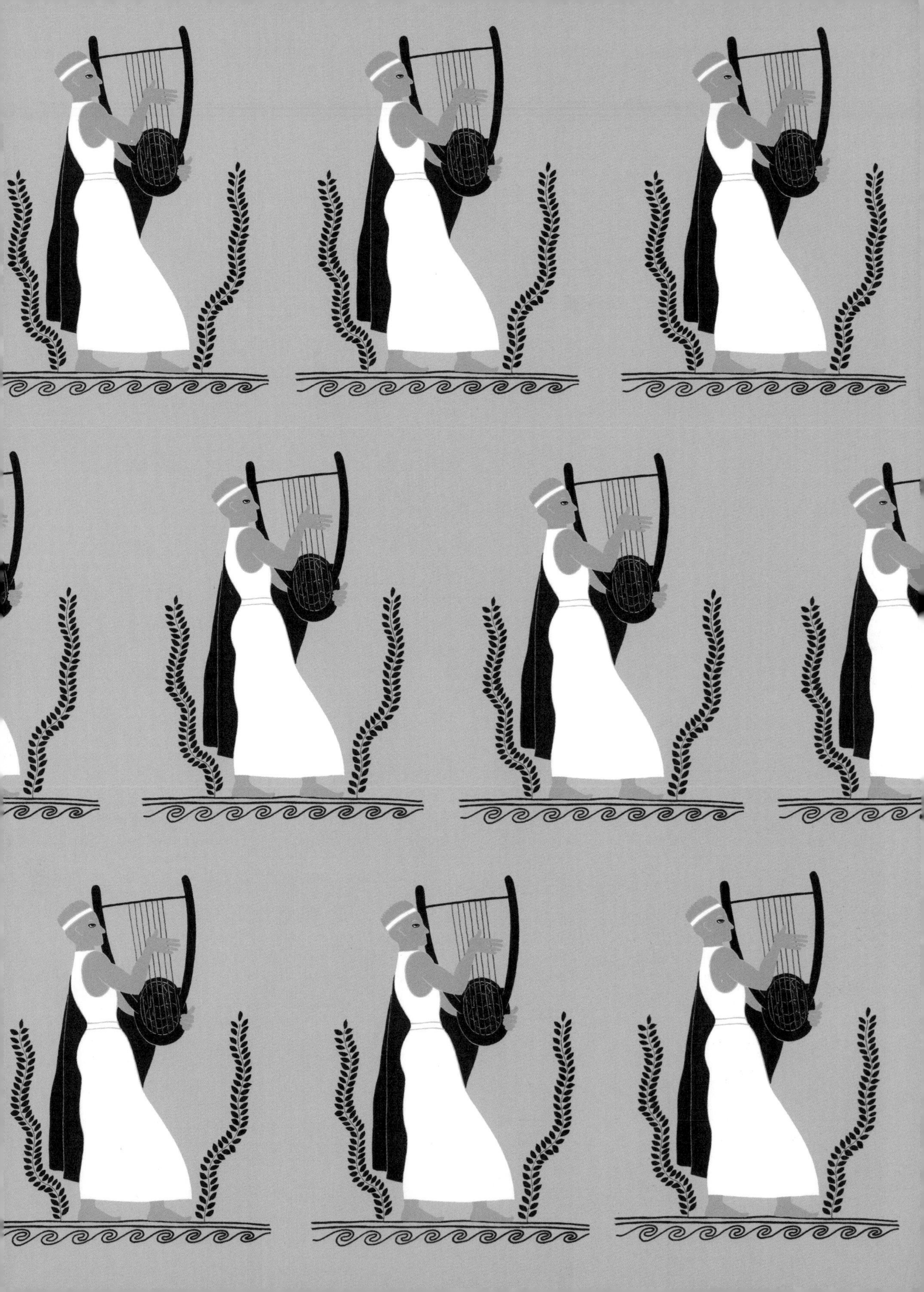